THE COLOR MONSTER

a story about emotions

ANNA LLENAS

L B

LITTLE, BROWN AND COMPANY
NEW YORK BOSTON

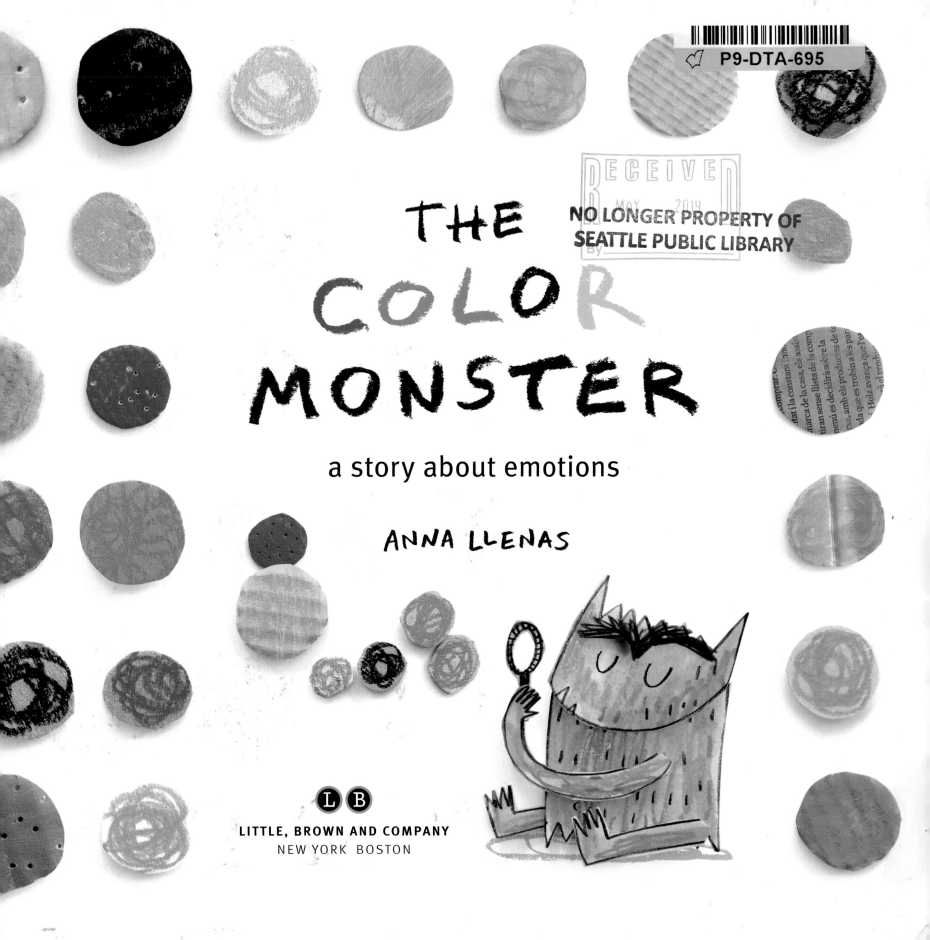

This is the Color Monster.

Today he woke up feeling confused,
and he doesn't know why.

Are you all mixed up again,
Color Monster?

Your emotions don't work well
when they're all jumbled up.

You should try to separate them,
and put each one in its own jar.
If you'd like, I can help you.
Let's try to make sense of how you feel.

This is happiness.
It shines yellow like the sun and
twinkles like the stars.

When you're happy,
you laugh and jump and dance and play!
You want to share your happiness with everyone.

This is sadness.
It is lonely and blue like a rainy day.
It washes over you like the sea.

When you're sad,
you hide and want to be alone.
You don't want to do anything...
except maybe cry.
It's okay to cry, Color Monster!

This is anger.
It burns red like a fire and
is hard to stamp out.

When you're angry, life can feel unfair.

Sometimes, you want to take out your anger on others.
But I'll be nice to you, Color Monster, and your anger will disappear!

This is fear.
It hides and runs away like
a mouse in the night.

When you're afraid, you feel tiny.
You think you don't have the
courage to face the gray shadows.
But I can help you find your way.

This is calm.
It is quiet like the trees and as light as
green leaves swaying in the wind.

When you're calm,
you breathe slowly and deeply.
You feel at peace.

Now you can rest, Color Monster!
All your feelings are in the right place.
See? Don't you feel much better?

Uh-oh...I see you're feeling
something new.

You look different, Color Monster!
Tell me...how do you feel now?

To my family and friends,
to all the colors living together